GUINEA PIG

PET SHOP PRIVATE EYE

#5

Raining Cats and Detectives

COLLEEN AF VENABLE

ILLUSTRATED BY STEPHANIE YUE

GRAPHIC UNIVERSE™ • MINNEAPOLIS • NEW

Story by Colleen AF Venable

Art by Stephanie Yue

Coloring by Hi-Fi Design

Lettering by Grace Lu

Graphic Universe™
A division of Lerner Publishing Group, Inc.
241 First Avenue North
Minneapolis, MN 55401 U.S.A.

Website address: www.lernerbooks.com

Library of Congress Cataloging-in-Publication Data

Venable, Colleen AF.
    Raining cats and detectives / by Colleen AF Venable ; illustrated by Stephanie Yue.
        p.   cm. — (Guinea Pig, pet shop private eye ; #5)
    Summary: When guinea pig Sasspants leaves Mr. Venezi's pet shop to live with Detective Pickles, and hamster-detective Hamisher retires, the other animals must try to solve the case of the missing bookstore cat without their help.
        ISBN 978–0–7613–6008–7 (lib. bdg. : alk. paper)
        ISBN 978–0–7613–8737–4 (eBook)
        1. Graphic novels. [1. Graphic novels. 2. Mystery and detective stories. 3. Guinea pigs—Fiction. 4. Hamsters—Fiction. 5. Pet shops—Fiction. 6. Animals—Fiction. 7. Humorous stories.] I. Yue, Stephanie, ill. II. Title.
    PZ7.7.V46Rai 2012
    741.5'973—dc2   2011021626

Manufactured in the United States of America
3 - 45364 - 11394 - 9/25/2020

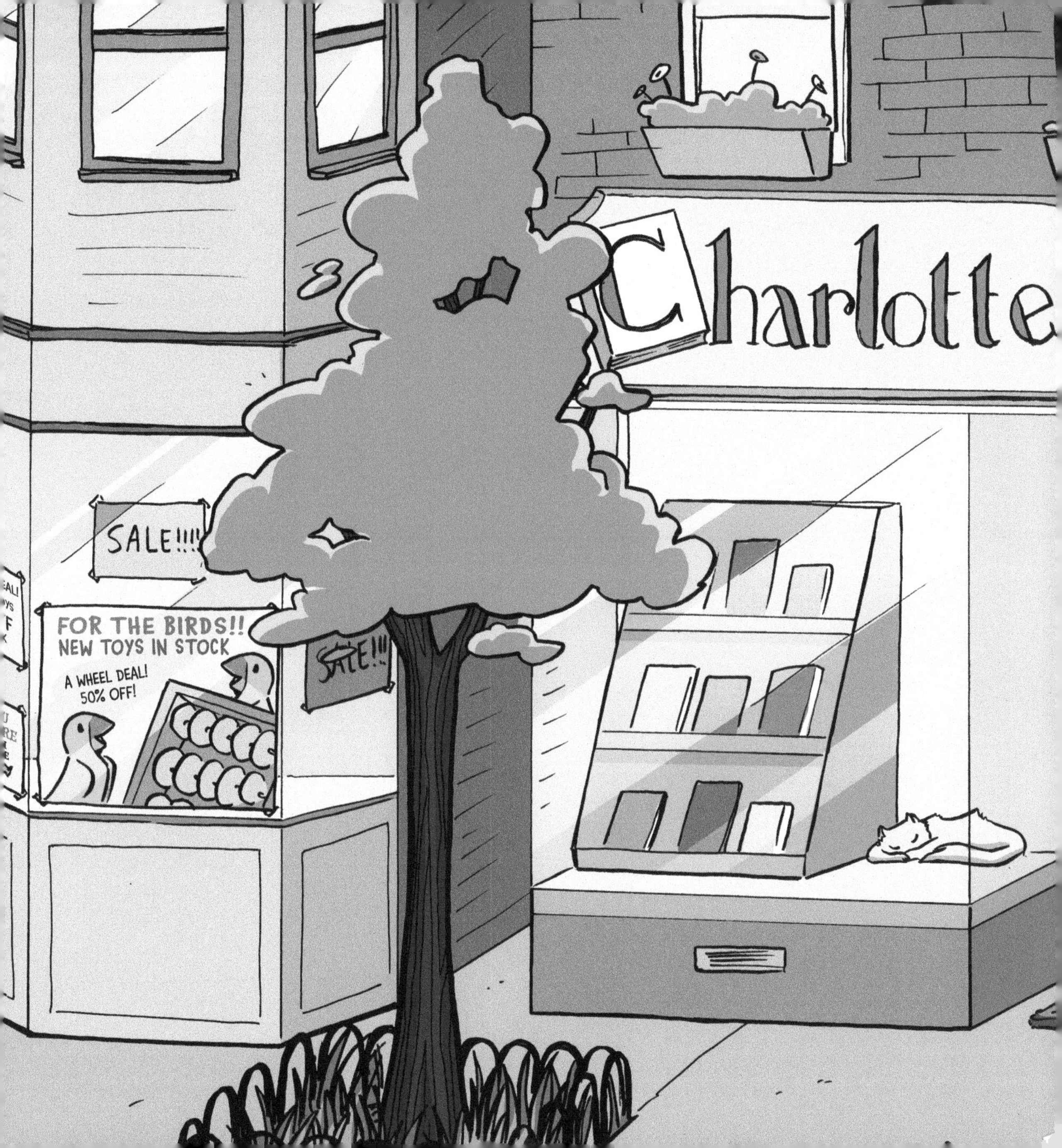
8
Charlotte
SALE!!!!
FOR THE BIRDS!!
NEW TOYS IN STOCK
A WHEEL DEAL!
50% OFF!
SALE!!!

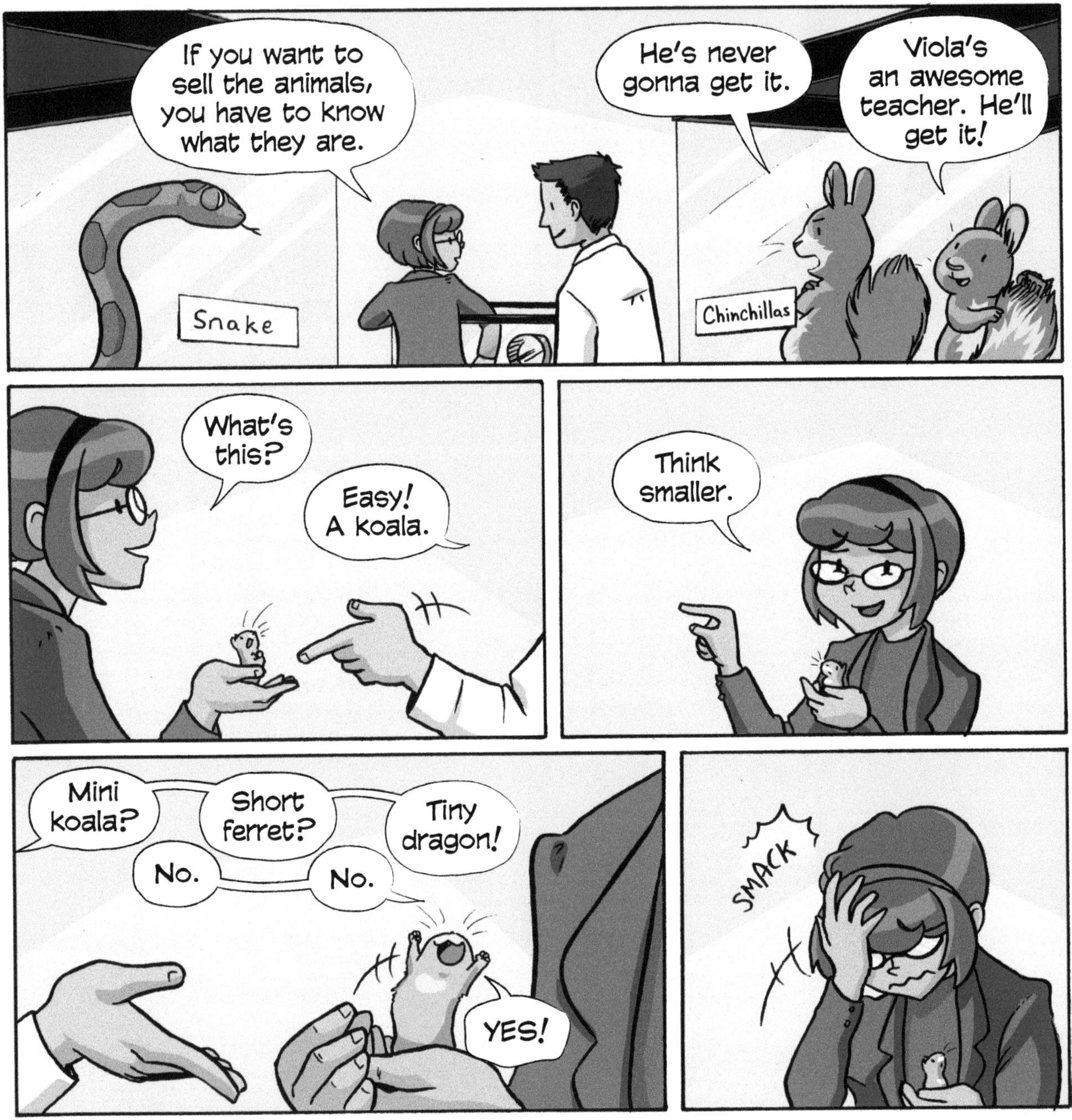
If you want to sell the animals, you have to know what they are.
Snake
He's never gonna get it.
Viola's an awesome teacher. He'll get it!
Chinchillas
What's this?
Easy! A koala.
Think smaller.
Mini koala?
No.
Short ferret?
No.
Tiny dragon!
YES!
SMACK

How about this one?

I'll give you a hint: It rhymes with RAKE.

HAMSTER!

Mr. V's getting so much better! Did you hear him call me a dragon?

SNAKE. How does "hamster" rhyme with "rake"?!

They both have A's in them?

He does seem to be trying. Viola isn't half bad.

What? I'm allowed to change my mind.

Ugh! We're done for today.

My brain feels bigger already. I hope my favorite hat will still fit.

SNAP!

5

Did you hear that Viola is going to buy Janice, Clarisse, and Mr. Sparkles as soon as she's saved up the money?

Really?

But Viola keeps spending her paychecks on tiny clothes and facial hair.

Facial hair?

I'm sorry Mr. V still can't get your name right, but I come with gifts. Who wants to be an itty-bitty Abe Lincoln?

Oh! Oh! Me!

So cute!

...And on yesterday's episode, Mandy and Clive were supposed to get married, but SHE'S still in love with his evil twin, who is pretending to be the caterer so he can put hot sauce in the wedding cake!

Gasp!

I hope my new owner is that awesome! And I bet whoever picks you will be super cool too. Maybe our owners will even live in the same state! We could see each other every few years!

Yeah.

I made you something.

Huh?

Detective Team:
MUST be Bought Together!

As if I'd let us live in different states.

You know, we really need a better detective office.

Oooh! With, like, a desk and file cabinets and a swimming pool with a diving board and a robot butler to answer the door if we're in the pool when somebody knocks and pens! OMG, we should have a cup full of pens!

Maybe we should just start by building a desk.

Yeah. I don't know where we're going to find all those pens.

Want to go to the bookstore and get some building materials?

Sure!

So what kind of owner do you want?

Oh, I'm not picky.

I just want someone who's a supercool professional detective, with a detective's hat and a detective's notebook and big ears to hear crime...

...and their favorite color is green and they've seen the movie THE SMALLEST MERMAID at least 10 times and know all the words and they have a last name that's also a noun, like Detective Cash or Detective Shoe or Detective Smallestmermaid.

Hey, look outside! It's the mice from the bakery!

Mmmm. Bread crumbs!

Aaah!

Don't worry. Tummytickles is totally harmless. He's Charlotte's cat.

Whoa! Has he always been here?

No. A week ago he used to be over here.

About an inch over here to be exact.

He's always sleeping.

I'm awake.

Aaah!

Ow. Tell the koala to stop yelling.

He's not a... never mind. Hi, Tummytickles.

Ugh. That's not my name. That's just what Charlotte's niece calls me. My real name is...zzzzz.

He's never awake long enough for me to find out.

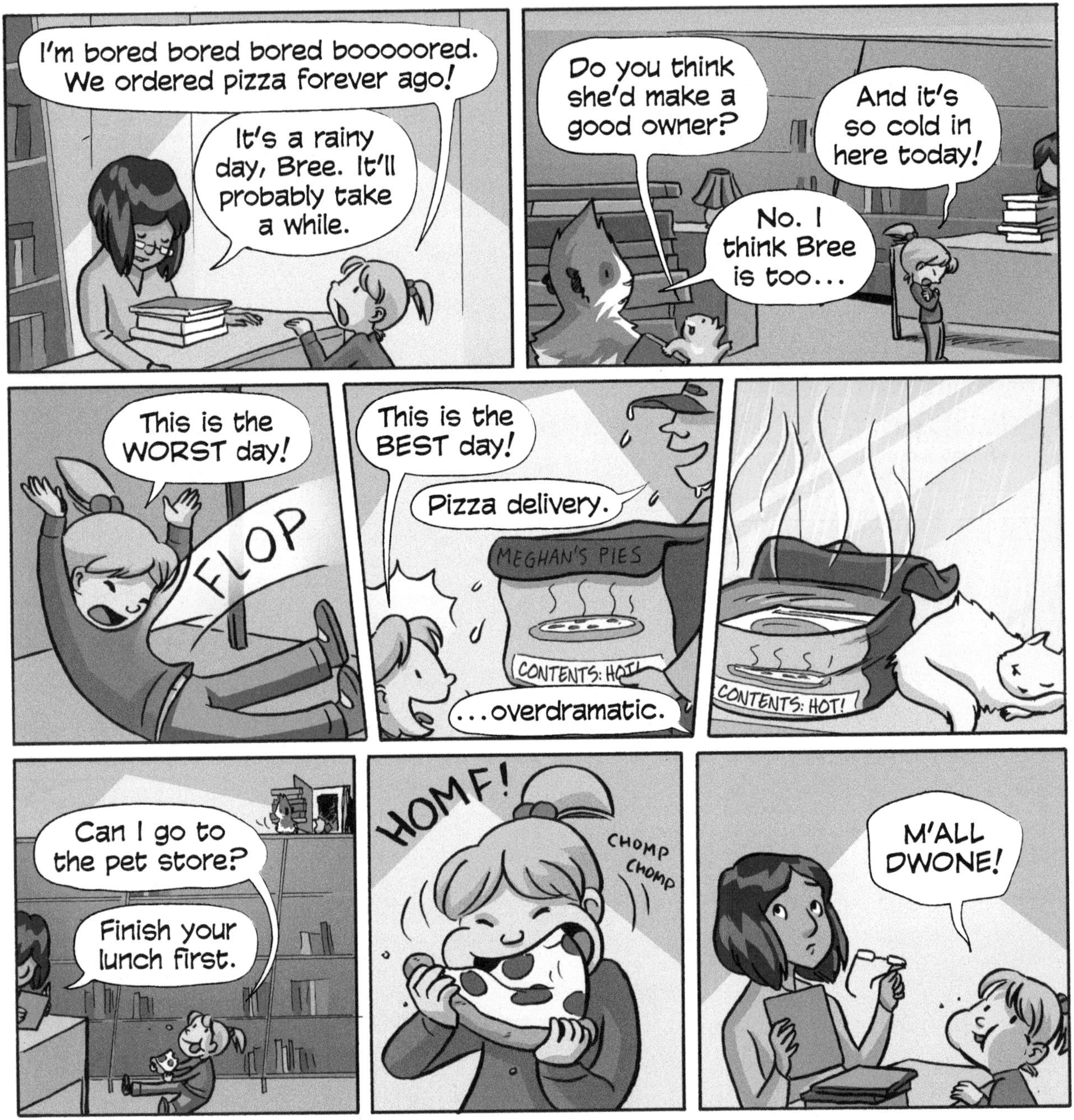
I'm bored bored bored booooored. We ordered pizza forever ago!
It's a rainy day, Bree. It'll probably take a while.
Do you think she'd make a good owner?
No. I think Bree is too...
And it's so cold in here today!
This is the WORST day!
FLOP
This is the BEST day!
Pizza delivery.
MEGHAN'S PIES
CONTENTS: HOT!
...overdramatic.
CONTENTS: HOT!
Can I go to the pet store?
Finish your lunch first.
HOMF!
CHOMP CHOMP
M'ALL DWONE!

What are you reading, Detective Pants and Sidekick Snack?

These are for building. We're making a desk and a robot butler!

KNOCK KNOCK!

Bree, don't tap the glass. Hi, Marcus.

Hi, Charlotte.

KNOCK KNOCK!

KNOCK KNOCK!

Someone get the door!

Orange you glad I didn't say orange!

Don't do it, Mr. Chicken! Stay on your side of the road!

But you DID say Orange.

Hwwwwelp. Mee.

I don't get it.

I've been practicing! This is a rabbit.

Uh...

Whooooooa.

That running wheel is HUGE.

DIBS!

I fell off my stupid bike in the stupid rain, and the wheel came off! This is going to cost so much to fix.

I almost had enough to buy the chinchillas too.

Stupid rain.

I wish I could give you a raise, but I keep getting these annoying bill things.

You could give Viola commissions.

I thought the Commissioner was busy with that bat guy?

"Commission" means that Viola would get part of each sale she makes.

That sounds like a great idea! From now on, I'm giving you a Commissioner.

Thanks, Mr. V! Thanks, Charlotte!

I'm gonna go find the Commissioner!

Uh...

The fish tell THE BEST JOKES! Can I buy them?

Huh? Huh? Huh? Huh? Huh?

I like Bree. She's funny. We should go live with Bree!

Don't forget our list. We're not being bought by anyone who doesn't fit the list.

Bree, you already have a cat. And fish don't talk.

Do too.

I guess I should throw this wheel out.

Hey!

Doesn't she care about dibs?!

Where's she taking the wheel?

Not fair! It took me forever to put on these running pants!

What?

There! The desk is done.

I'm working on files!

I'll make a file for everyone who comes into the shop. We can use it for cases or to figure out if someone will be a good owner!

MR. VENEZI

tall(er than me), not-fluffy, eyes: two, mouth: one

Nice work! Hey, I have a gift for you.

A CUP OF PENS?!?! How did you do that?!

Mr. V is always losing pens on the floor. There were more, but they wouldn't fit.

I got something for our office too!

Ta-da!

It's a file cabinet for our case files.

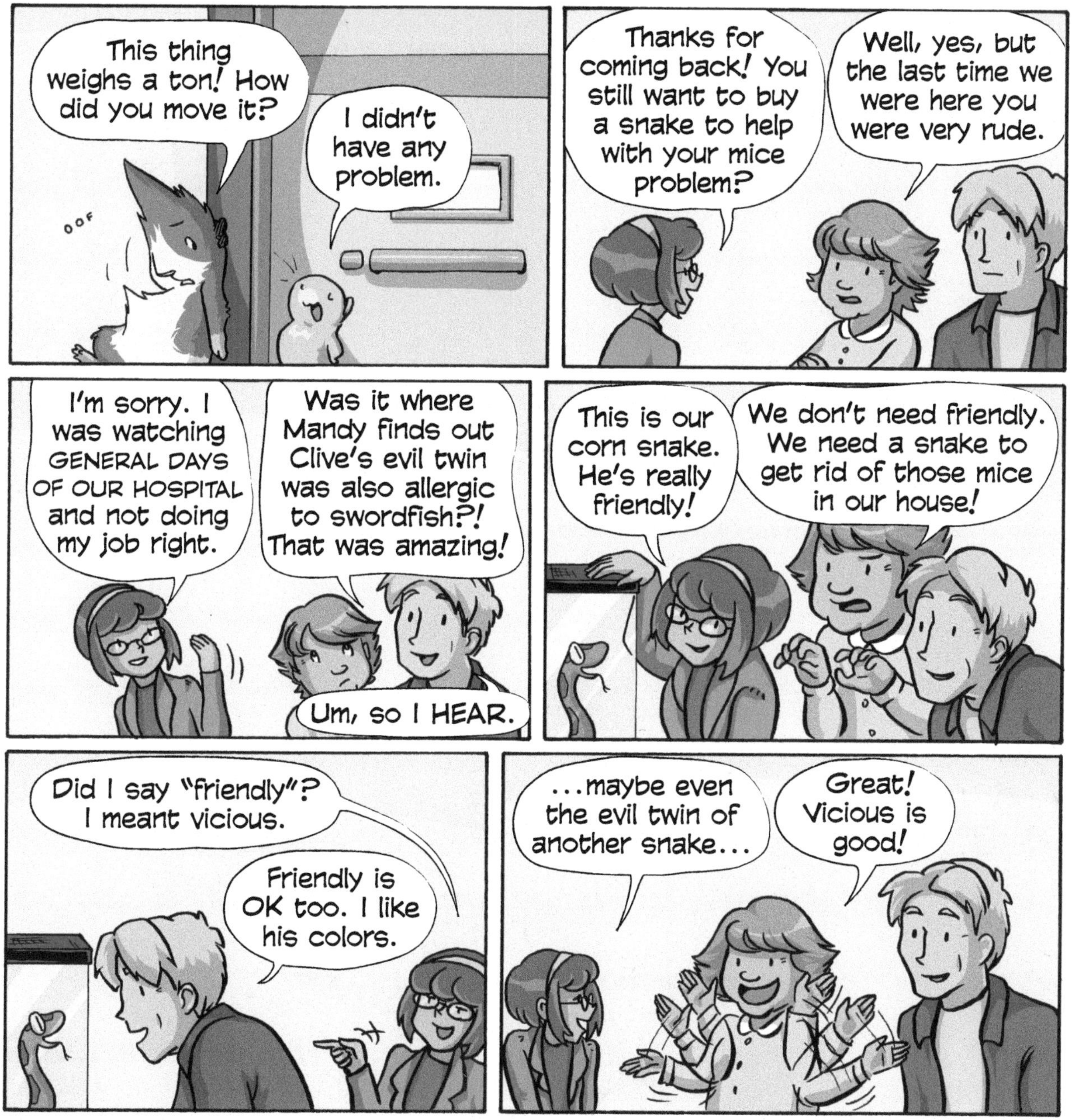
This thing weighs a ton! How did you move it?
OOF
I didn't have any problem.
Thanks for coming back! You still want to buy a snake to help with your mice problem?
Well, yes, but the last time we were here you were very rude.
I'm sorry. I was watching GENERAL DAYS OF OUR HOSPITAL and not doing my job right.
Was it where Mandy finds out Clive's evil twin was also allergic to swordfish?! That was amazing!
Um, so I HEAR.
This is our corn snake. He's really friendly!
We don't need friendly. We need a snake to get rid of those mice in our house!
Did I say "friendly"? I meant vicious.
Friendly is OK too. I like his colors.
...maybe even the evil twin of another snake...
Great! Vicious is good!

How's the character file coming?

Tell that lady to stop moving her arms.

We'll take it!

It's going to be so odd with Gerry gone. He's always been here.

SKTCH SKTCH

LADY AND MAN!

Eyes: Four
Mouths: Two
Arms: Twenty-Seven (Estimated)
Personality: Nice
Taste in TV shows: Bad
Thoughts: Good owners for Gerry!

You'll get rid of all those mice, won't you?

Knock knock!

Bye, everyone.

Good-bye, Gerry!

See ya!

We're saved!

What? Who? Where?

I'll miss you, Sasspants. You were always my favorite.

I'll miss you too.

Yay! Gerry found the perfect owner! I should update the files! I hope our owner shows up soon.

Hamisher, the likelihood that someone who fits your long list would walk through that door is...

TUG TUG

What?

DETECTIVE!

Arms, Legs, Mouth: Doesn't matter as long as he/she is nice!
Looks: Big ears
Last name: Noun
Likes: Green and movies about singing half-fish people
Personality: Smart, kind, wears a cool hat
Thoughts: Great owner for Sasspants and Hamisher!

cume in
OPEN

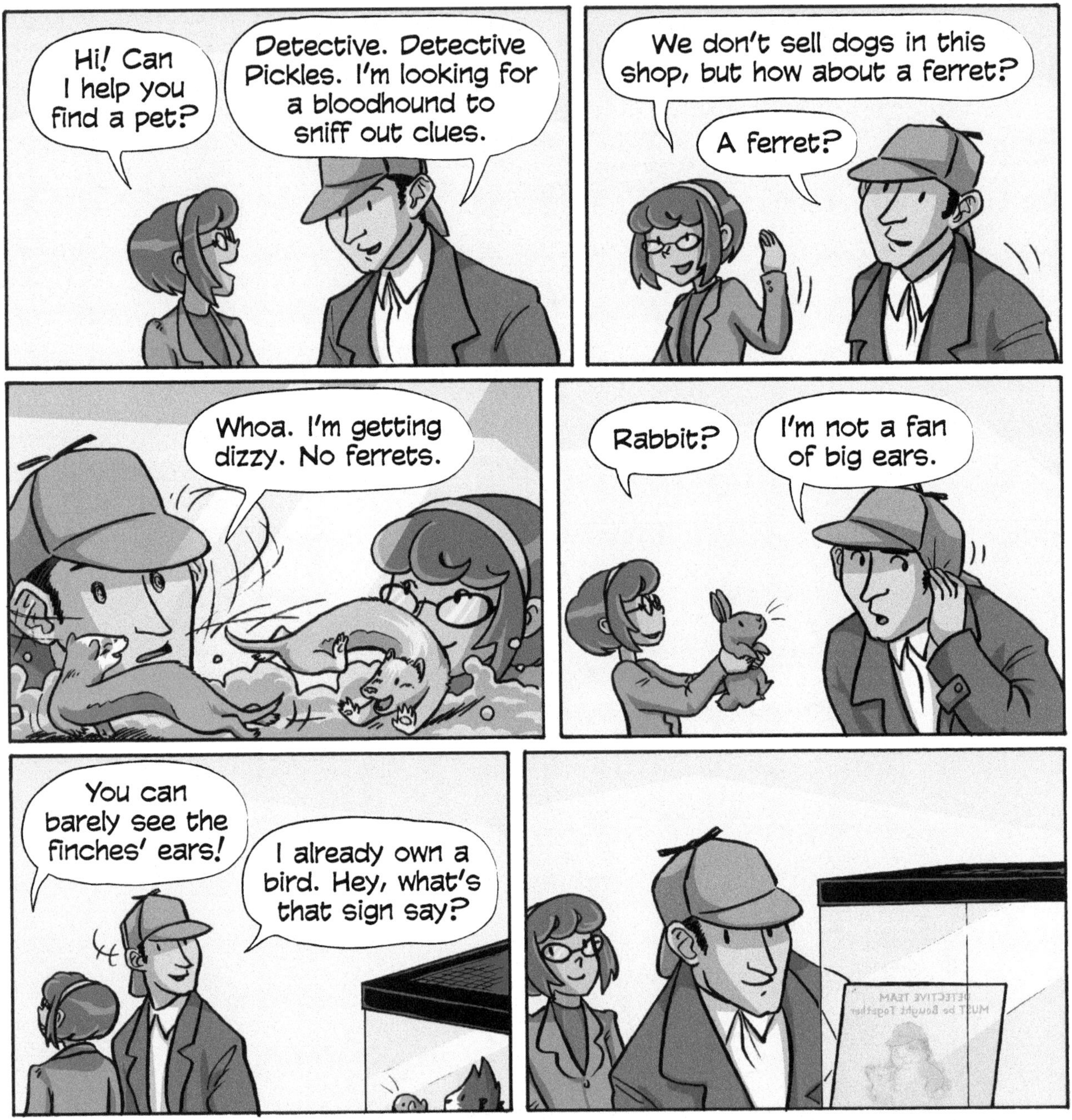
Hi! Can I help you find a pet?
Detective. Detective Pickles. I'm looking for a bloodhound to sniff out clues.
We don't sell dogs in this shop, but how about a ferret?
A ferret?
Whoa. I'm getting dizzy. No ferrets.
Rabbit?
I'm not a fan of big ears.
You can barely see the finches' ears!
I already own a bird. Hey, what's that sign say?
DETECTIVE TEAM
MUST be Bought Together

I've always wanted a guinea pig. And what's that? A gerbil?

It's a hamster. Gerbils have tails.

Dragon!

She's a really smart guinea pig, even if every day is a bad hair day for her.

Ha ha. Sasspants has bad hair.

Shhhh!

You know what. I'll take them!

Great!

5 cents, 6 cents, 7 cents...

...35 cents, 36 cents...

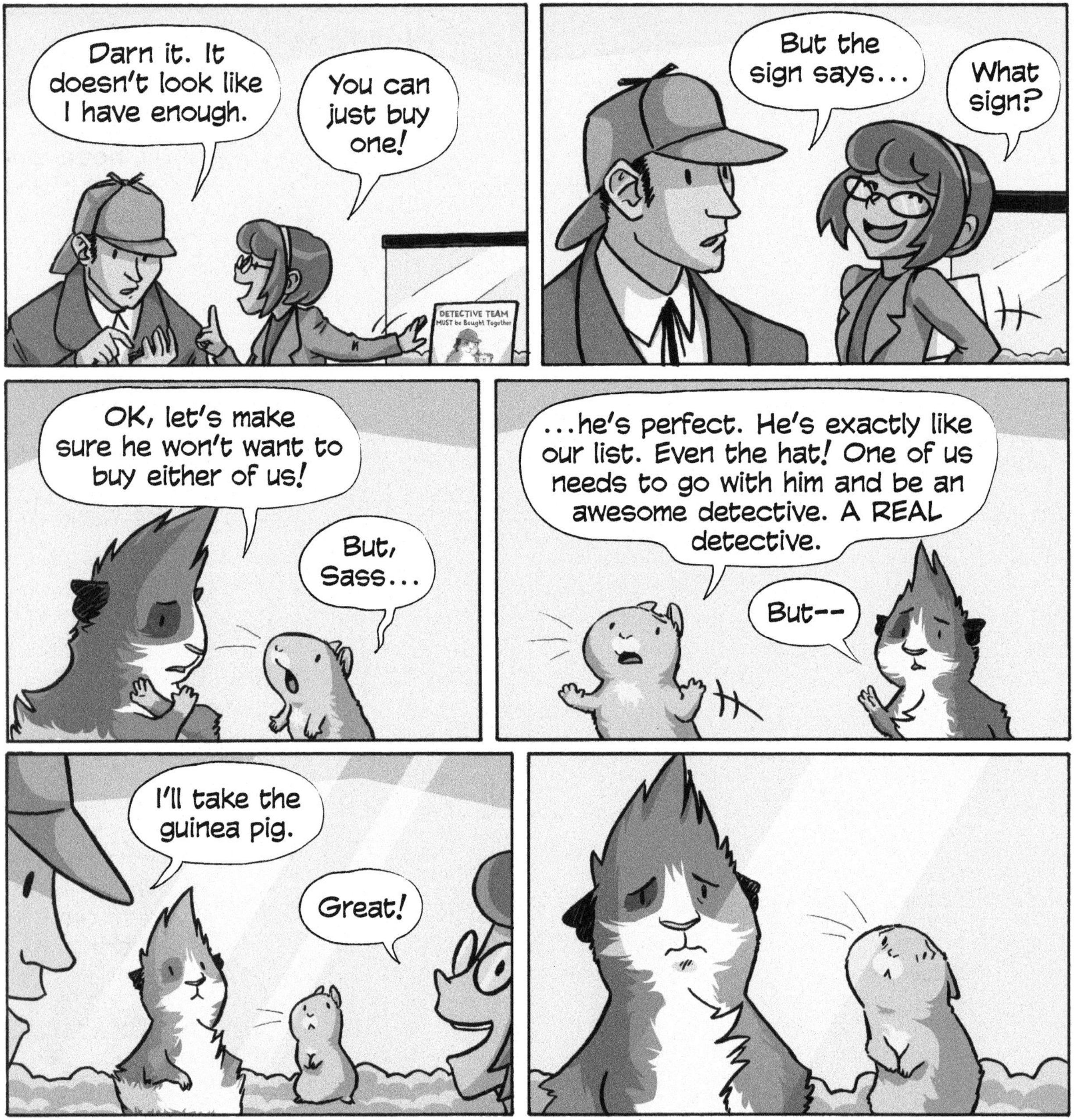

Darn it. It doesn't look like I have enough.
You can just buy one!
DETECTIVE TEAM
MUST be Bought Together
But the sign says...
What sign?
OK, let's make sure he won't want to buy either of us!
But, Sass...
...he's perfect. He's exactly like our list. Even the hat! One of us needs to go with him and be an awesome detective. A REAL detective.
But--
I'll take the guinea pig.
Great!

"I have the perfect place for her in my huge library filled with books."

"Go on! You'll be happy!"

"When he has enough money, you can come back for me!"

"He does seem nice and smart."

"Don't forget his hat!"

"OK, I'll do it."

"Great."

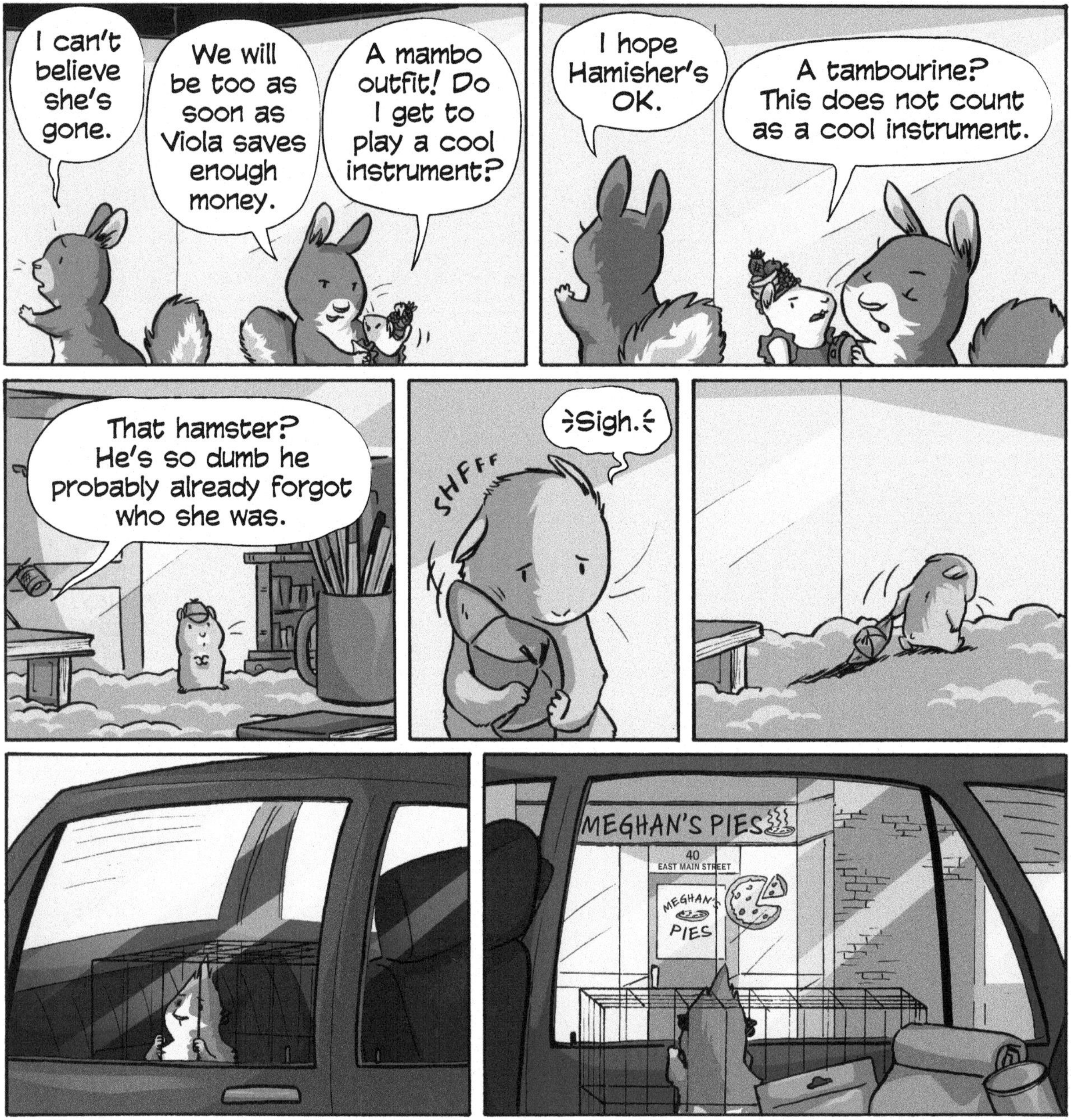
I can't believe she's gone.
We will be too as soon as Viola saves enough money.
A mambo outfit! Do I get to play a cool instrument?
I hope Hamisher's OK.
A tambourine? This does not count as a cool instrument.
That hamster? He's so dumb he probably already forgot who she was.
SHFFF
Sigh.
MEGHAN'S PIES
40
EAST MAIN STREET
MEGHAN'S
PIES

Welcome home! I hope you like it.

Wow.

These are Lizz, Evan, Mike, Cory, Marianne, and Steve. And our bird friend here is named Polygon.

Hi!

Awk! Polygon want a cracker. Awk!

Here's a spot for you, but I'll leave the door open so you can come and go as you please.

I would play, but I really am more into reading silently and solving cases. I hope you can understand.

This is... nice.

THE POSTMAN ALWAYS BRINGS MICE

CLIMB AND PUNISHMENT

CLIMB AND PUNISHMENT
A History of Thievery on Mount Everest

Meanwhile, back in the shop...

Hi, Detective Dragon!

I'm not a dragon. Or a detective. I'm just ⋛SIGH⋚ a hamster.

But what about Steve?

We can't find Steve!

Here I am!

Wow! You found yourself!

You should be a detective, Steve.

Steve's right behind you, Steve!

Detective Steve!

BING BONG

Viola, have you seen our cat? We can't find him anywhere!

I haven't seen him.

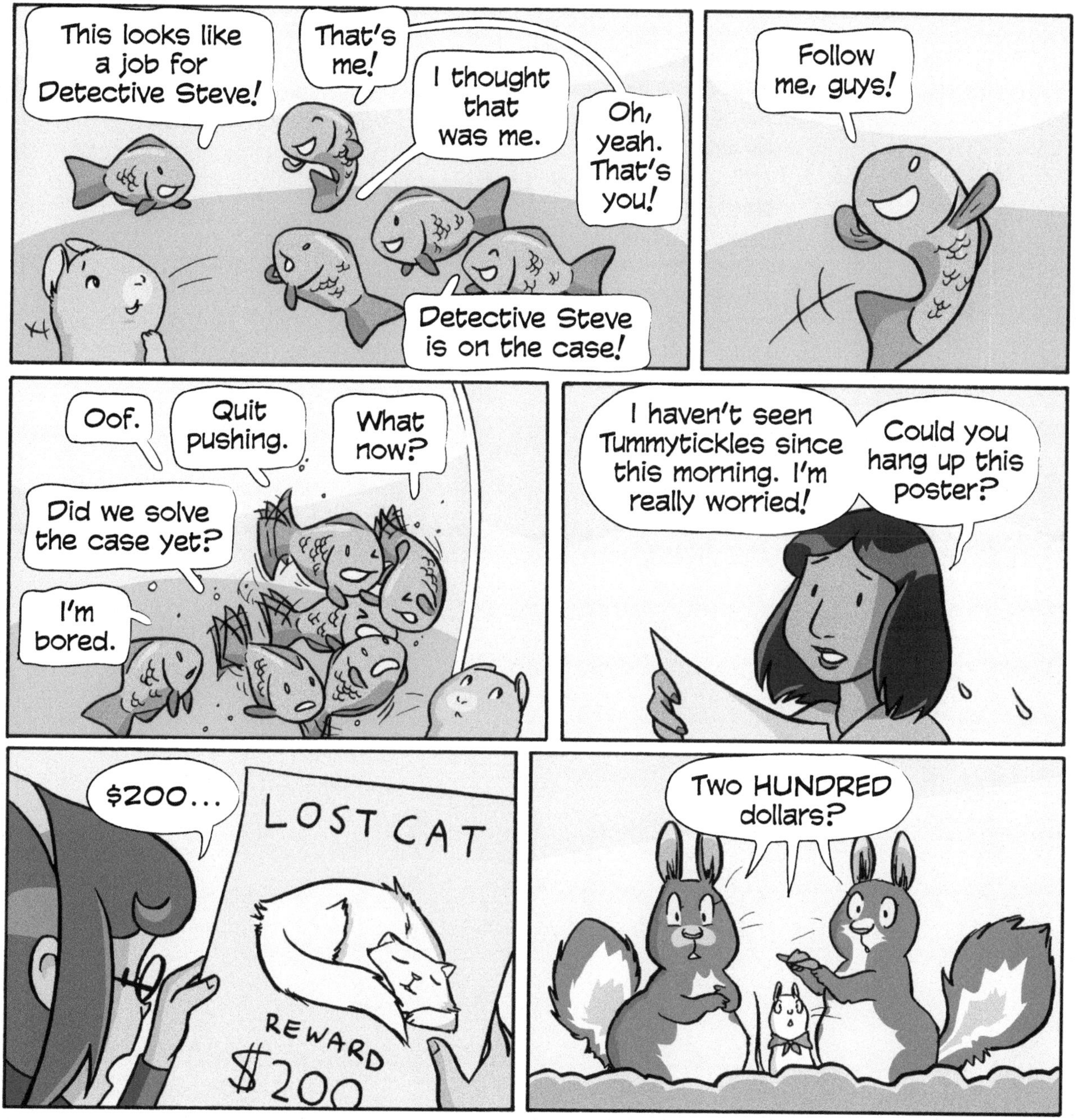
This looks like a job for Detective Steve!
That's me!
I thought that was me.
Oh, yeah. That's you!
Detective Steve is on the case!
Follow me, guys!
Oof.
Quit pushing.
What now?
Did we solve the case yet?
I'm bored.
I haven't seen Tummytickles since this morning. I'm really worried!
Could you hang up this poster?
$200...
LOST CAT
REWARD
$200
Two HUNDRED dollars?

Back at Detective Pickles' house...

He'll bore you with blueprints. I'm Cory, fish of action. I'm almost done with my time machine.

I'm Lizz. With two z's. Just finished my first novel. Want to see my Pulitzer?

Hi, I'm Evan. Are you interested in building humanoids? I've got this idea for a robot butler...

Hi. I'm Sasspants.

Mike. Architect. I'd show you my recent work, but you wouldn't understand it.

Hello! Bonjour! ¡Hola! Jambo! I'm Marianne. Name a language. I bet I can speak it!

What, you thought since we're goldfish, we can't also be smart?

I like bread!

Shhhh. Quiet, Steve!

What about you?

I only say that silly "Polly want a cracker" line because it's an ironic play on the typical role of parrots in our society.

Also, I really like crackers.

So what kind of cases has Detective Pickles solved lately?

Well...none.

He's waiting for...

...a big one.

He doesn't want to waste his genius...

...on something beneath him.

I guess that makes sense.

Besides, there are a lot of less important detectives who can take silly cases. Remember the stolen sandwich?

Ha ha! The sandwich!

That pet store guy kept phoning! Too funny! Who cares about a stolen sandwich?

Back in the pet shop...

How does this detective hat look?

Sasspants never wore a detective hat.

She didn't have any style. We're going to find that missing cat, and then Viola will buy us with the reward money!

27

Are you guys trying to be detectives?

Not TRYING. We ARE detectives. And we're going to find the missing cat!

I bet Sasspants would have found him already. She's the greatest detective who ever lived.

Sigh. We miss her!

Yeah. Me too.

Whatever! We're already better detectives than that guinea pig ever was!

No way. I bet Herbert could find the cat before you!

A hat? I don't wear hats. They mess up my hair. I'm scared of bowler hats.

I don't think hats should be playing sports at all.

I bet we can find the cat before Herbert does, or anyone else in this pet shop!

Which reminds me of the time...

Did you hear? Clarisse challenged everyone in the pet shop to find the cat before she does!

I'm not a detective anymore.

Oh, I know. I just wanted to ask if I could borrow your detective hat.

SIGH.

Thanks!

You ready for me to turn the page?

Riiiiiiiing

Darn. Right when we got to a good part.

Hello. This is Detective Pickles. What's your case?

A missing bookstore cat?

Is it a special cat? One of a kind? Worth a fortune? Does it talk? Hmmm. Just a regular old cat? What's its name? Tummytickles?

Tummytickles?

Sorry, this doesn't sound like an important case, and I'm very busy. Good luck.

Now, where were we...?

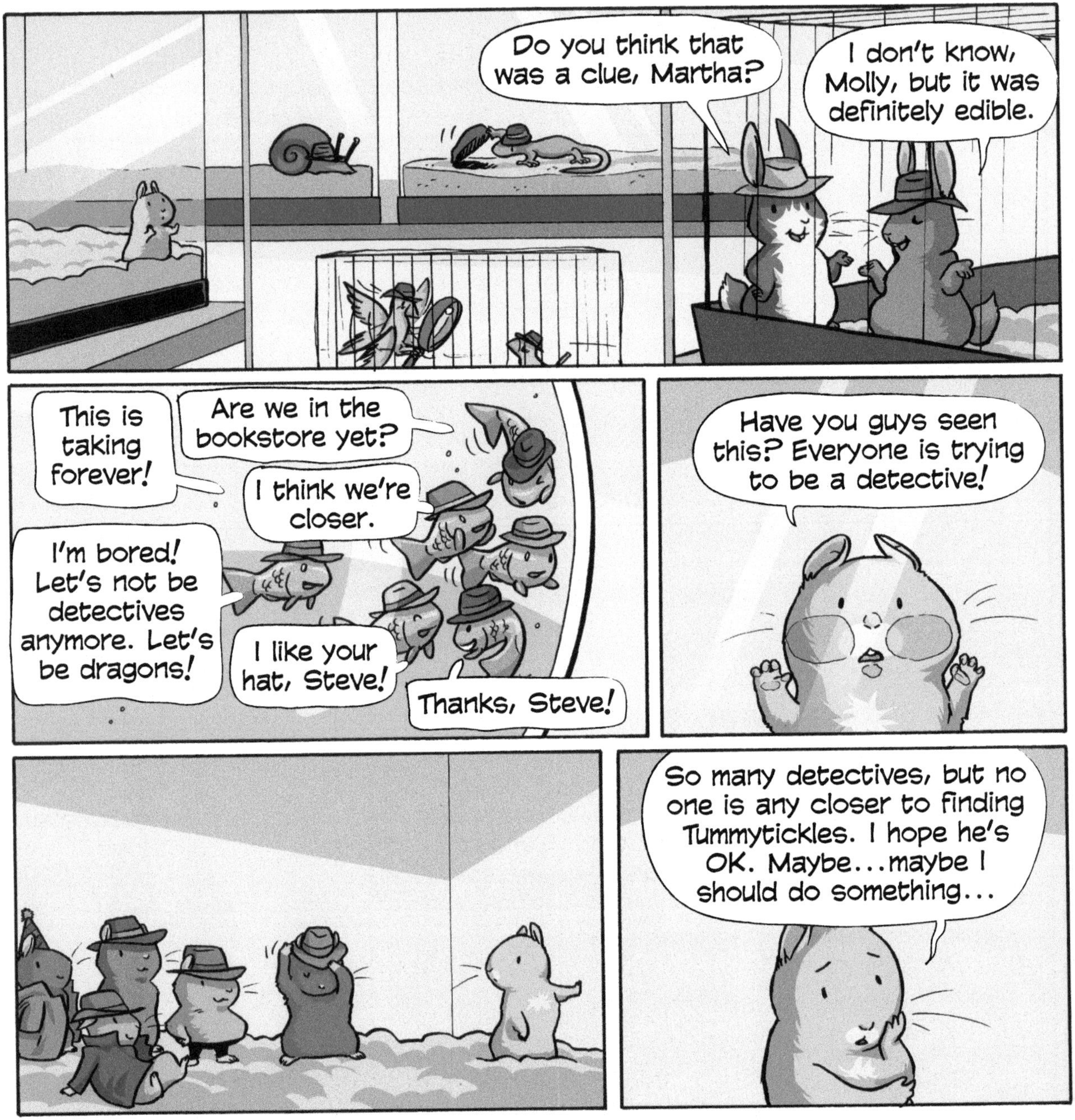
Do you think that was a clue, Martha?
I don't know, Molly, but it was definitely edible.
This is taking forever!
Are we in the bookstore yet?
I think we're closer.
I'm bored! Let's not be detectives anymore. Let's be dragons!
I like your hat, Steve!
Thanks, Steve!
Have you guys seen this? Everyone is trying to be a detective!
So many detectives, but no one is any closer to finding Tummytickles. I hope he's OK. Maybe...maybe I should do something...

Whatcha up to, Sasspants?

One of my friends is missing, and if no one else is going to help, I need to.

The cat from the phone call?

Can't a cat find his own way home?

All he has to do is find a computer.

Cats run the Internet.

Aaah! Cat? Where?!

Don't you like it here?

Detective Pickles is so nice, I've never seen so many books, and you guys are all so smart. But this isn't my home.

KREEEEEK

CRANK

FLUFF!

Wait with us for a real case, like a missing diamond or kidnapped president!

I thought we were friends.

We ARE friends.

But not best friends. I already have one of those.

31

TUCK

Oh, good! Cats. Maybe they have an idea where Tummytickles might be.

Hey, guys, do you have a minute to help me out? See, my friend is missing her cat and...

...and...

Thirty seconds later.

Geesh. I just wanted to talk.

Whoa. That was awesome.

I know YOU! You're that guinea pig from the pet shop!

I eat bread crumbs at the bakery every morning. The mice are always talking about how cool you are!

Wow! I can't believe I'm meeting Detective Pants!

Well, I...

Wait! You were outside yesterday morning when Tummytickles went missing!

Tummytickles?

The bookstore cat. Do you remember who went into the store?

It was so rainy I would have stayed home, but those bagel bits are so tasty and stale. Delicious.

Don't mind Earl. He'll fly anywhere for food. He's even been to First Street! That's a whole five blocks!

Maybe the cat just ran away?

Tummytickles doesn't even move, let alone run. How does a cat who doesn't move go somewhere?

Oof. This was a lot easier with Sasspants!

OK, clues. Gotta find clues. I can do this! So Tummytickles usually sleeps here, but sometimes he sleeps...

...here.

Ugh, too bright! I need some shades.

Charlotte won't mind if I borrow these. I hope I don't get weird tan lines.

Aw, man, this is so hard! There are no clues, and it's way too warm here!

Wait...warm. Tummytickles likes to sleep where it's warm!

Hmm. What else is warm? Hot tubs. Jelly beans you find in your pockets. Robots left on too long. Pies.

Someone had to carry Tummytickles out of the bookstore. How could someone do that without being seen, and who...

I've got it!

Earl! Do you know where to find pizza crusts?

Of course. I am a pigeon of high taste.

The trash bin behind Meghan's Pies is a gourmet gem.

Can you take me there? Um. Not the trash bin. The front door is fine.

My hat itches. Do I have to wear it?

Yes! Until we find this cat! Let's go over the suspects.

Well, so far you've suspected the cat thief to be Gerry, Sasspants, Hamisher, the ferrets, the lizards, all of the fish except for Steve, the rabbits, the mice next door, the mail lady, yourself, Mr. Sparkles, and former president Richard Nixon. All of whom, minus the last one, were proven innocent.

Being a detective is a lot harder than it looks. I hope Herbert isn't doing any better.

In order to find a cat, I should start to think like a cat. Meow. Meow. Meow. Meow. Which reminds me of the time I meow. Meow. Meow.

Maybe this bet was a bad idea.

Why are you still so sad? We're supposed to sell the animals.

But that koala and zebra were my favorites.

I only sold the zebra. I'm sure the koala-- I mean, the hamster will turn up.

Geesh, you have me doing it now too! Let's practice. What's this?

Eggplant.

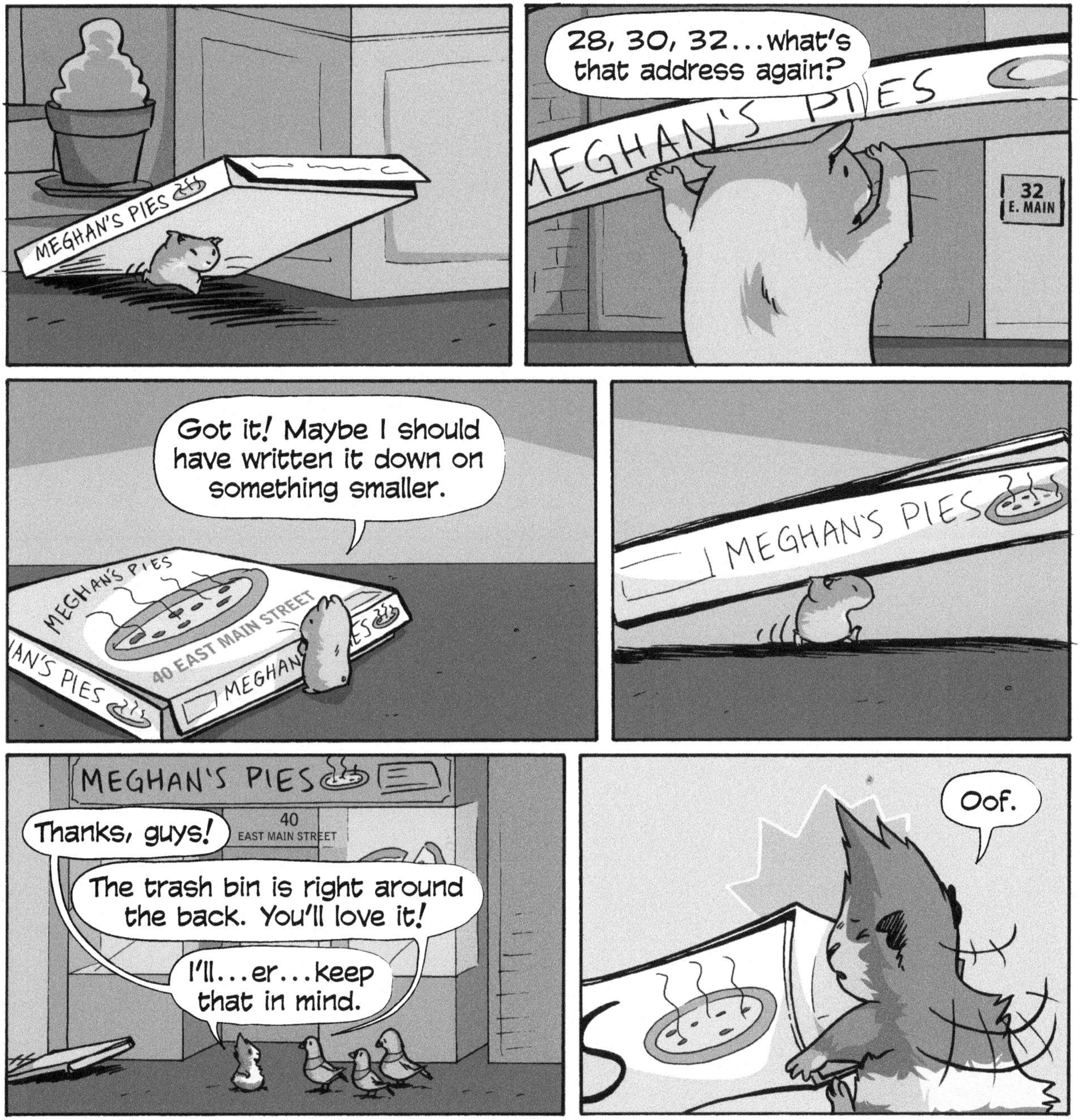
MEGHAN'S PIES
28, 30, 32...what's that address again?
MEGHAN'S PIES
32 E. MAIN
Got it! Maybe I should have written it down on something smaller.
MEGHAN'S PIES
40 EAST MAIN STREET
MEGHAN'S PIES
MEGHAN'S PIES
Thanks, guys!
40 EAST MAIN STREET
The trash bin is right around the back. You'll love it!
I'll...er...keep that in mind.
Oof.

Hamisher?

Sass!

Who were they? Your new best friends?

Just some pigeons who helped me out.

You left me.

You told me to leave you!

But I didn't mean it!

Why aren't you at the detective's house?

I missed my friends. I missed my BEST friend.

Also, I'm pretty sure I figured out what happened to Tummytickles.

Me too!

Want to take a peek?

MEGHAN'S PIES
CONTENTS: HOT!

There he is!

MEGHAN'S PIE

MEGHA

How'd you figure it out?

He likes to sleep in a warm place, and it was so cold in the bookstore that day. I figured out that he must have climbed in the bag, and the delivery guy didn't notice!

And I figured out that someone had to carry him away, since he doesn't exactly like to move. The pizza guy was the only person in the shop that day.

ZZZ
MEGHAN
CONTENT
wiggle wiggle

Hey, wake up.

Geesh, he's heavy!

YAAAWN

STREEETCH

I'm awake. Where'd all the rectangle things go?

You aren't in the bookstore. We're here to take you back.

Oh. You guys want a lift?

Woo!

Um...I don't know.

Come on! It'll be fun, and we'll get there faster!

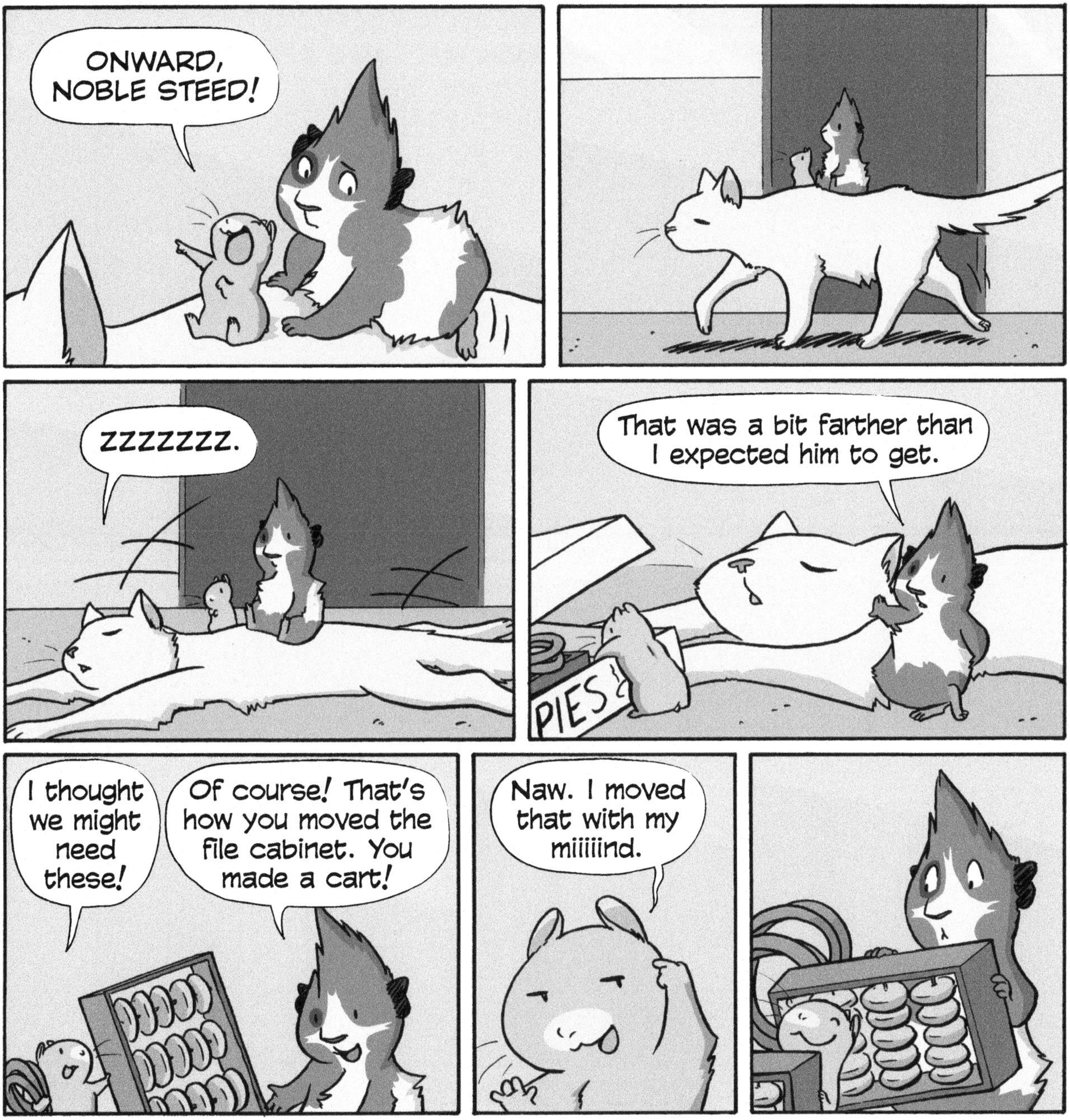
ONWARD, NOBLE STEED!
ZZZZZZZ.
That was a bit farther than I expected him to get.
PIES
I thought we might need these!
Of course! That's how you moved the file cabinet. You made a cart!
Naw. I moved that with my miiiiind.

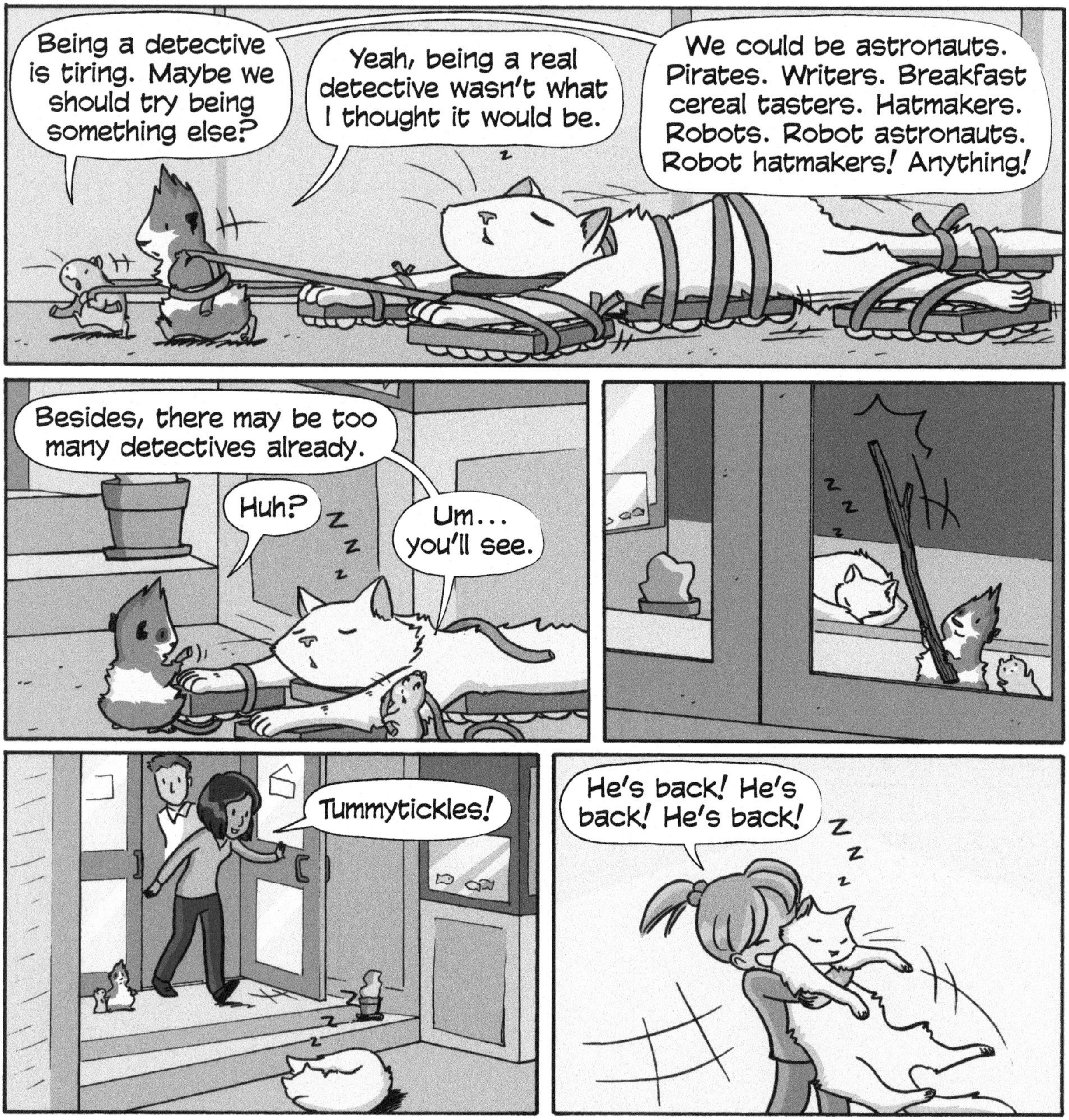
Being a detective is tiring. Maybe we should try being something else?
Yeah, being a real detective wasn't what I thought it would be.
We could be astronauts. Pirates. Writers. Breakfast cereal tasters. Hatmakers. Robots. Robot astronauts. Robot hatmakers! Anything!
Besides, there may be too many detectives already.
Huh?
Um... you'll see.
Tummytickles!
He's back! He's back! He's back!

Darn it! WE wanted to find him!

Why is everyone dressed as a detective?

Long story.

I'm a dragon, and fire comes out of my nose!

Knock knock!

I'm a nose, and dragons come out of my fire!

HMMOOO'S MAAARE?

THAT'S an even longer story.

Thank you so much for helping keep me calm today, Marcus. It meant a lot to me.

It's no problem at all.

SMACK!

Um...Charlotte... do you maybe want to go out on a...

I want a refund on this snake! He doesn't eat mice at all. In fact I keep catching him PLAYING with them.

YES WE'RE OPEN

Not a word.

What? I didn't say anything.

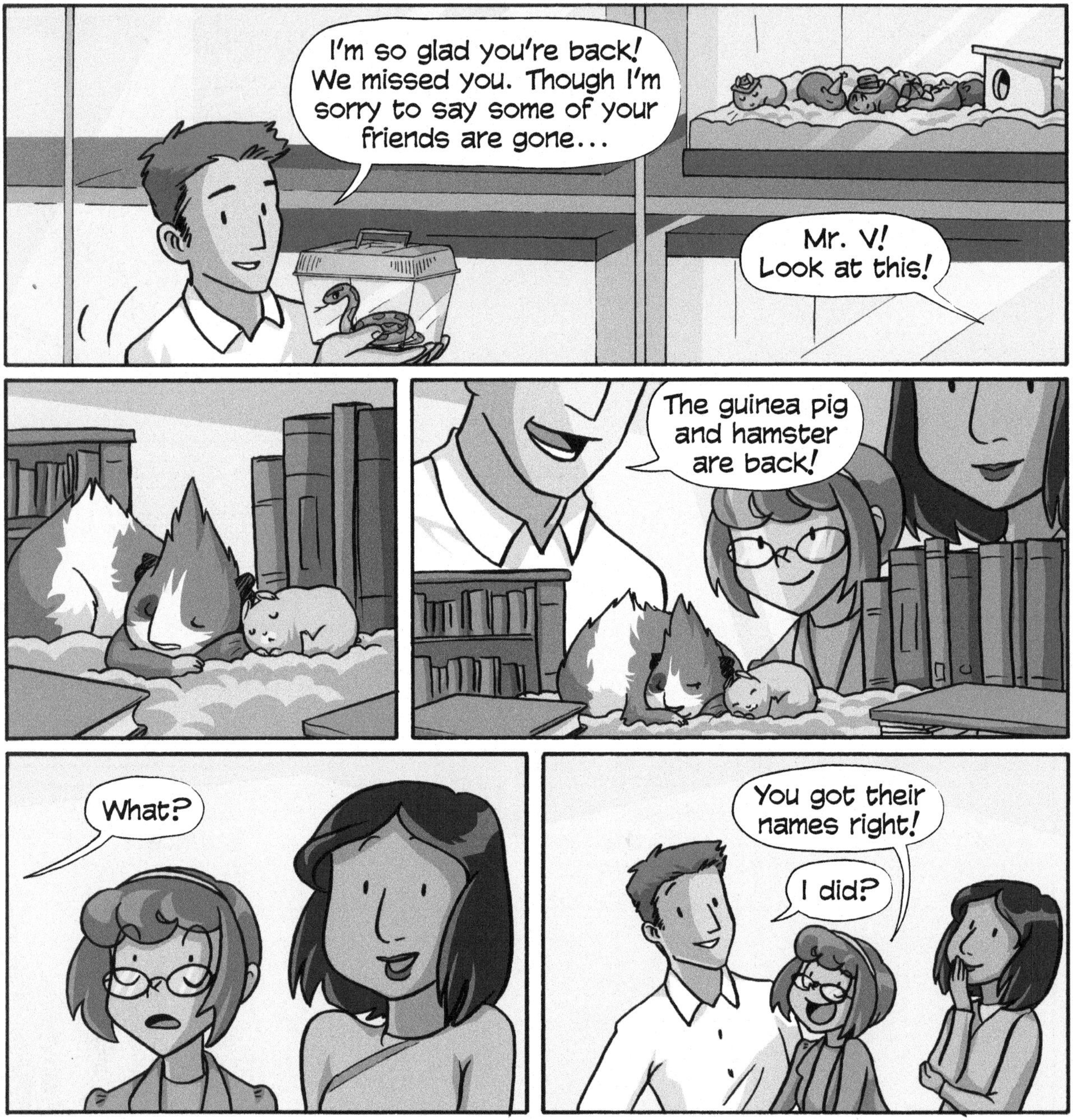
I'm so glad you're back! We missed you. Though I'm sorry to say some of your friends are gone...
Mr. V! Look at this!
The guinea pig and hamster are back!
What?
You got their names right!
I did?

You know, I don't think I want to say good-bye again.

Maybe you can just sell pet food and toys and not sell the animals?

But what about the chinchillas and the mouse? I've been saving to buy them!

Nope. You can't buy them.

WHAT?!

They're yours. Consider it a Commissioner Gordon.

Commission.

Both of those things.

Thank you! Thank you!

Can you say yay, Tummytickles? Yaaaaay!

Detective. Detective Pickles here. The guinea pig that I bought from this shop has gone missing, and I'm here to sniff out...

...clues...

Hmm. Case closed.

Aw. I am going to miss her.

No time for mushy stuff. The pig stays where she's happy. Give me my refund in the form of a can of fish food, a parrot toy, and one guinea pig treat for her.

I have a feeling she's had a long day.

So if we aren't detectives anymore, what are we?

Anything we want to be.

THE END!

HAMISHER EXPLAINS...

CATS!

It's hard to believe that Tummytickles is related to tigers, lions, and the cheetah—the world's fastest land animal—since domestic cats sleep around 17 hours a day. If you have a 10-year-old cat, he's probably spent 7 of those years totally asleep! BUT cats can run 30 miles per hour, while very fast humans can only run about 27 miles per hour.

Not all cats are as lazy as Tummytickles. Some even have jobs. Humphrey was a stray cat hired by the British government in 1989 to keep the prime minister's office mouse free. Humphrey was given an official government title, Chief Mouser to the Cabinet Office, and even had a yearly salary! There have been cats in the White House too. Abraham Lincoln was the first president to own a house cat, but the ACTUAL first cats to live in the White House were a pair of tiger cubs owned by President Martin Van Buren. Eep! He was a president with really silly facial hair. Almost makes you wonder if he had a tiger as a barber!

Domestic cats come in all different colors and breeds, but if you want to tell two cats apart, look at their noses. Cat noses are like human fingerprints and have little ridges that form patterns. No two cat noses are exactly the same!

Cats are the most popular pet in the world, but they didn't always hold that title. In China around 500 B.C. it was illegal for anyone other than the emperor to own a cat. In the 1400s, the Catholic Church officially denounced cats, because people believed cats were connected to witches. Eventually people realized that having more cats around means fewer rats around and fewer rats means fewer plagues!

A lot of famous people throughout history have loved cats. Leonardo da Vinci painted the smiling Mona Lisa, but he also loved drawing cats and said they were a "masterpiece" in the world of nature. Sir Isaac Newton figured out what gravity is, but he also invented the cat door so his cat, Spithead, could come and go as he pleased.

A group of cats is called A TERRIFYING THING FOR A HAMSTER TO SEE...or also a "clowder." A group of kittens is called a "kindle"!

The BEST Animal Detectives!

While Herbert and the fish may not have made the best detectives, there are a lot of animals that would look really good in detective hats...and would make pretty good detectives too.

MASTER OF DISGUISE:

MIMIC OCTOPUS: Totally the stealthiest animal! Not only can they change their skin color in a few seconds to blend in with any background, but they're named "mimic" because they have the ability to imitate over 15 other animals including water snakes and fish. The mimic octopus is one of the only animals in the world that is that smart and it's definitely the fastest at putting on its disguises!

BEST SNIFFER OF CLUES:

BLACK BEAR: Bears may not take that many showers, but they smell great! Actually, in the animal kingdom, they have the most powerful noses of all. Bears can smell things from over 20 miles away. Their sense of smell is seven times better than a bloodhound's and over 2,000 times stronger than a human's! If detectives were really smart, they'd use bears instead of dogs to sniff out clues...um...or maybe they made the right decision.

MOST OBSERVANT:

JUMPING SPIDER: They get their name from their ability to jump over 40 times their body length, but it's their eyes, all EIGHT of 'em, that make jumping spiders awesome detectives! Jumping spiders have four sets of eyes, and each set works like a fancy spy camera: one set for seeing things far away, one set for sensing movement on their sides, one set that can measure distances, and even a set that has special night vision. Ooooh.

BIGGEST SMARTY-PANTS
(NOT TO BE CONFUSED WITH SMARTY SASSPANTS)

Some scientists say CHIMPANZEES are the smartest, and others say DOLPHINS. Both are great at puzzles, learn spoken commands, and love playing games and sports. If I had to pick which would make better detectives, I'd have to say chimpanzees...mostly because they wouldn't keep losing their hats.

WHAT ANIMAL DO YOU THINK WOULD MAKE THE BEST DETECTIVE?